Based on the TV series *Nickelodeon Avatar: The Legend of Aang*™ as seen on Nickelodeon

First published in Great Britain in 2008 by Simon & Schuster UK Ltd
Africa House, 64-78 Kingsway, London WC2B 6AH
A CBS Company

Originally published in the USA in 2008 by Simon Spotlight,
an imprint of Simon & Schuster Children's Division, New York

A CIP catalogue record for this book is available from the British Library

ISBN: 978-1-84738-240-5

Printed in the USA

10 9 8 7 6 5 4 3 2 1

Visit our websites: www.simonsays.co.uk
www.nick.co.uk

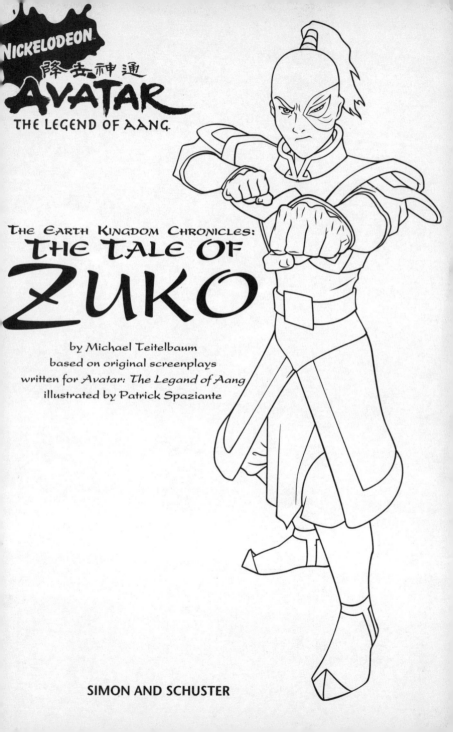

AVATAR
THE LEGEND OF AANG

THE EARTH KINGDOM CHRONICLES:
THE TALE OF
ZUKO

by Michael Teitelbaum
based on original screenplays
written for *Avatar: The Legend of Aang*
illustrated by Patrick Spaziante

SIMON AND SCHUSTER

Chapter 1

My name is Zuko. I am a prince of the Fire Nation and heir to the throne. As of now, however, I'm a prince in exile. My father, Fire Lord Ozai, has banished me—at least until I can deliver the Avatar to him. This scar on my face, given to me by my own father, is merely an outward sign of my humiliation. The true pain of my exile runs much deeper.

So far I have failed to capture the Avatar. But I must succeed, for along with his capture comes the return of my honor, my birthright, and most important of all, my father's respect. I am the older of his two children and it is my destiny to follow my father onto the throne as Fire Lord. But that will never come to pass unless I can redeem myself.

Following our terrible defeat at the hands of the Avatar during a huge battle at the North Pole, my uncle Iroh and I escaped on a home-made raft. After three weeks at sea, clinging by a thread to our very lives, we landed at a resort in the Earth Kingdom. Here we will rest and recover while I plan my next step.

Today is a very sad day. While my uncle, who is fond of his creature comforts, gets a  massage, I can think only of the fact that three years ago on this day my father ordered me to leave the Fire Nation.

"It's the anniversary, isn't it?" Uncle asked.

"On this day three years ago I was banished. I lost it all . . . and I want it back!" But I don't know how to go about getting it. And so I wait and think.

My uncle doesn't care about my problems. As long as he has a full stomach, a hot cup of tea, and a comfortable bed, nothing else matters. He spends his days walking the beach, collecting useless seashells.

One evening after he had returned with a new sack full of shells, I got the shock of my life.

"Hello, brother, Uncle," said a voice from the shadows.

No, it can't be! Azula! My younger sister, here. But how? Why? And what does she want? All she's ever done is tricked me, humiliated me, and shown everyone that she's better than me—better at Firebending, and at gaining our father's affection. She was not the one banished from her home, so what could she possibly want from me?

"What are you doing here?" I shouted.

"What, no hello? Have you become uncivilized, Zu-Zu?"

"Don't call me that!"

I hate it when she calls me that. It's just another way of putting me down, making me feel like she's really the big sister and I'm just a little kid.

"I've come with a message from home," she began. "Father's changed his mind. Family is suddenly very important to him. Father regrets your banishment. He wants you home."

Did I just hear that correctly? Is it possible that Father wants me home? All of a sudden, all is forgiven? Can everything in my life change in a matter of seconds?

Now Azula is yelling at me, but I don't hear her. All I can think of is going home.

"Did you hear me?" I finally heard her shout. "You should be happy! Excited! Grateful."

I just can't believe that Father regrets what he did, and that he wants me back. I'm feeling something I haven't felt in three years: hope . . . and relief. I'm really going home!

At some point Azula left, but I didn't remember her going. This was before Uncle ruined the happiness I was feeling. "I have never known my brother to regret anything," he said. "If Ozai wants you back, it may not be for the reasons you imagine."

How can Uncle betray me like this? Why is he standing there shattering my dreams? "You don't know how my father feels about me. You don't know anything!" I snapped.

I wish he could let me enjoy my moment of redemption.

"You are a lazy, mistrustful, shallow old man

who has always been jealous of his brother!" I shouted, then I ran outside.

That's it then, isn't it? Uncle can't hope to be half the man that Father is. For these three years he's been trying to act like he was my father. But now that Father wants me back, Uncle is jealous. He doesn't want to give me up. Well, too bad. I'm not his son. I'm Prince Zuko, son of the Fire Lord, and I am going home!

I hurried away as quickly as I could, making my way toward Azula's ship. But as I walked, doubt began to creep into my mind, and I tried to fend it off.

Can I be wrong about Uncle? Maybe I'm being too harsh. He's always stuck by me no matter what. Maybe I'm judging him too quickly. He would make good company on the long voyage back to the Fire Nation, and—

I hear someone coming up behind me. It's Uncle!

"Wait!" he called, hurrying to catch up. "Don't leave without me!"

"You changed your mind!" He must realize that I'm right about Father, that he really does want me back.

"Family sticks together, right?" was all he said, and that was good enough for me. I'm glad he's here. "We're finally going home," I replied.

As we made our way onto the ship's gang-plank, Azula appeared on deck.

She's smiling. She has changed. She is glad to be bringing me back to Father. Maybe everything will work out for me after all.

"Brother! Uncle! I'm so glad you decided to come!" Then she turned to the ship's captain. "Set our course for home, Captain."

"Home." It was the most beautiful word.

"You heard the princess," the captain shouted to the crew. "Raise the anchors. We're taking the prisoners home."

It took me a while to realize what the captain had said. I saw the fury in my uncle's eyes before I fully understood that the captain had called us "prisoners." This was a trap after all!

Uncle blasted Azula's soldiers off the gangplank. "Run!" he shouted to me.

"You lied to me!" I yelled at my sister.

Azula simply laughed. "Like I've never done that before."

I'm such a fool for ever thinking she would do something to help me.

"You know Father considers you a miserable failure for not finding the Avatar," Azula continued. "Why would he want you back home except to lock you up where you can no longer embarrass him?"

She taunts me. It's obvious that she's enjoying my humiliation, just like she did when we were kids. I won't let her get away with it!

I fired a Firebending blast right at Azula, but she ducked out of the way and countered with an attack of blue lightning. My little sister has gotten strong. I hate to admit it, but maybe she's too strong for me. She dodges every attack and strikes back with incredible power. I don't know if I can beat her.

Uncle directed one of Azula's lightning blasts away from me, and the force of the blast knocked her overboard. This was our chance to escape.

We raced through the woods before finally stopping when we approached a river.

"I think we are safe here," Uncle said, glancing back over his shoulder.

Once again I am on the run—now as an outcast from my own people. Azula hurt me today, much more with her betrayal than with her Firebending. I am a fugitive, a desperate soul in hiding, with a lost past and no apparent future.

🌀 🌀 🌀

We wandered through the forest, and we had nothing to eat. "I can't live like this! I wasn't meant to be a fugitive!"

Then Uncle drank a tea he made from some wild berries and broke out in a horrible rash. "When the rash spreads to my throat, I will stop breathing."

Can our situation get any worse? "We need to get help," I told him.

"But where are we going to go?" Uncle asked as he scratched himself everywhere. "We're enemies of the Earth Kingdom and fugitives of the Fire Nation."

"If the Earth Kingdom discovers that we are Fire Nation, they'll get rid of us somehow," I pointed out. "But if the Fire Nation discovers us, we'll be turned over to Azula."

Just the mention of her name makes me

angry. I'm not ready to face her again. Not yet. "Earth Kingdom it is," Uncle agreed. It was the lesser of two bad options.

We disguised ourselves as Earth Kingdom citizens and headed into a village, where we found a hospital. They'll be able to help Uncle there.

In the hospital we met a nurse named Song who soothed Uncle's rash, then invited us to her home for dinner.

It's dangerous. We can't risk being found out. Still, I can't remember being so hungry. We'll have to keep a low profile, eat the food, and get out of there quickly.

"My daughter tells me you're refugees," Song's mother said as she served us. "We were once refugees ourselves."

"Really?"

"Yes," Song said. "When I was a little girl, the Fire Nation raided our farming village. All the men were taken away. That was the last time I saw my father."

I don't care to remember the last time I saw my father.

"I'm sorry," Song said. "What's wrong?"

"Nothing." My expression must have

betrayed my thoughts. "I haven't seen my father in many years either."

"Oh, is he fighting in the war?" Song asked.

"Yeah." The nurse had been very kind to us. What would she say if she knew who Father really was, if she knew what he had done to her father? I couldn't sit here and eat their food. "I'm not very hungry," I said.

I went outside to think . . . alone. But Song followed me.

"Can I join you?" she asked, and she sat down beside me without waiting for a reply. "I know what you've been through. We've all been through it. The Fire Nation has hurt you."

What's she doing? She's lifting her hand and reaching for my face. She's going to touch my scar. No! I pushed her hand away.

"That's okay," she said. "They've hurt me too."

She showed me her leg, and there was a scar like mine: a burn mark, caused by a Fire-bender, that was all over her leg. What have we done? This girl meant no harm, yet she has suffered. She—stop it, Zuko! You're getting soft. Maybe coming here was a bad idea.

I did not know how to respond to Song, but was determined to leave right away.

"Thank you for the duck," Uncle said. "It was excellent."

No more pleasantries. Let's just go, Uncle.

"Where are your manners?" Uncle chided me as I headed out. "You need to thank these nice people."

"Thank you," I said quickly. They are our enemies. I don't need to thank them for anything.

"I know you don't think there's any hope left in the world," Song said.

Why won't she leave me alone? I don't need this girl feeling sorry for me.

"But there is hope," she continued. "The Avatar has returned!"

The Avatar. Another reminder of my failure. "I know," I replied without feeling. Now can we just leave?

Finally they went back into the house—and it looks like we got lucky. An unguarded ostrich-horse was tied to a tree. This is convenient, and it will get me away from here much faster. I'll just untie it.

"What are you doing?" Uncle whispered nervously. "These people just showed you great kindness."

"They're about to show us a little more kindness." I climbed onto the ostrich-horse. "They just don't know it yet." We are Fire Nation. We take what we need and don't look back.

Uncle just stood there, hesitating. He is weak. He is soft. "Well?" I asked impatiently. Then he climbed on behind me. Good, now we can leave. Good riddance.

Chapter 2

I feel lost in limbo. We ride on this beast from town to town, but with no plan, no direction, and at the moment, no food. And so now we find ourselves in the humiliating situation of sitting here in the marketplace of a small village begging for coins. I hate this! I just hate it.

"Spare coins for weary travelers?" Uncle called out to each person walking by. Some toss coins into his basket, others don't.

"This is humiliating! We're royalty. These people should be giving us whatever we want."

"They will," Uncle replied. "If you ask nicely."

That's not what I meant! Imagine me, a prince of the Fire Nation, reduced to this. Things can't get any worse than they already are.

Just then a man came up to us, waving a gold coin at Uncle. "How about some enter—tainment in exchange for a gold piece?" he asked.

How dare he! What are we, trained animals singing and dancing for our supper? "We're not performers," I said. This guy should just move along before I make him regret the fact that he ever saw us.

What's Uncle doing? I can't believe it. He's standing and singing for this guy.

"Let's see some action!" the man yelled, before pulling out two swords.

"Dance!" he shouted.

Now he's swiping the swords at Uncle's feet. Uncle is dancing to stay out of the way. I would blast this guy with Firebending in a heartbeat if it wouldn't blow our cover.

"Ha! Nothing like a fat man dancing for his dinner," the man said, laughing. Then he tossed the gold coin into our basket.

I'm totally humiliated, but Uncle doesn't seem the least bit embarrassed.

"Such a kind man," Uncle said.

I can't take this anymore. Maybe I can't stop the humiliation in the middle of a crowded market, but that doesn't mean I can't do anything about it.

That night I put on a blue mask to hide my identity. Moving quickly across the rooftops, I looked down into a dimly lit alley and spotted the man who had forced Uncle to dance.

Perfect!

Down I dropped, taking the arrogant fool by surprise. I knocked him down and he dropped his swords. I snatched them up quickly and flashed them in front of the man's face. He scrambled to his feet and dashed away. Now I have a disguise—and two excellent weapons! Hmm . . . that gives me an idea.

If those who have plenty won't give me what I want, I'll simply take it—or rather, my alter ego, the Blue Spirit, will take it!

There's someone carrying baskets of food. Those baskets look like they belong to me. I'll just swoop down on these foolish peasants. If my mask doesn't scare them, my swords will!

There! I have freed the food from the grasp of these peasants, and it is now mine. I feel better already. But I can't let Uncle know I'm doing this. He'll go on about right and wrong and I'll never hear the end of it.

I hid the mask and swords in the trees, then delivered my bounty.

"Here!" I said, tossing the food to Uncle.

"Where did you get this?" he asked suspiciously.

20

I knew he would give me a hard time. "What does it matter where they came from?" When have you ever questioned free food, old man?

Over the next few days I brought many treasures to Uncle at our hideout in the woods. Food, blankets, gold, jewels, all liberated from their former owners by the Blue Spirit.

I like taking what I want without asking permission.

"Zuko, I think we should talk," Uncle said when I had returned with a large sack of gold and food and a new teapot for him. "I know we've had some difficult times lately. We've had to struggle to get by. But it's nothing to be ashamed of. There is a simple honor in poverty."

Honor? How can he speak of honor? Has he forgotten so soon? "There is no honor for me without the Avatar."

"Zuko, even if you did capture the Avatar, I'm not so sure it would solve our problems. Not now."

Hard as it is for me to acknowledge this, I know that he is right. With Father now having placed his trust in Azula, even getting my hands on the Avatar might not be enough to satisfy him. "Then there is no hope at all."

Uncle leaped up and grabbed me by the shoulders. "No, Zuko! You must never give in to despair, to your darkest instincts. In the darkest times, hope is something you give to yourself. That is the meaning of inner strength."

Words. Just words. They mean nothing to me. Uncle can't possibly know how I feel. In fact, I can't see a good reason to continue traveling with him. I have lingered too long in his shadow. He slows me down. Him and his tea and his food and his comforts. No, it's for the best. I must do what is good for me.

"Uncle, I've thought a lot about what you said and it's helped me realize something. We no longer have anything to gain by traveling together. I need to find my own way." There, I said it. I feel better already, like a burden has been lifted. He's not saying a word. He's just looking away. Very well. I'll just go.

"Wait!" Uncle cried.

What? Now that he sees me leaving, is he going to try to talk me out of going? No. He's just giving me the ostrich-horse. Well, it will be easier than walking. I'll take it.

Thank you, Uncle. Good-bye.

I've always had to struggle, always had to fight, from the time I was a boy. It's made me strong, made me who I am. That's why I know I will survive, here, alone.

I rode the ostrich-horse into a small Earth Kingdom village. My stomach was grumbling and I felt light-headed, but I had to focus. I had to find food in this village.

"Could I get some water, a bag of feed for the ostrich-horse, and something hot to eat?" I asked a merchant as I held out my only two coins.

"Not enough here for a hot meal," the merchant said. "I could give you two bags of feed."

If animal feed is what I must eat to survive, then that is what I'll do. I nodded and handed him the coins.

I saw a little boy throw an egg at a group of Earth Kingdom soldiers, then run away. The soldiers approached me.

"You throwing eggs at us, stranger?"

"No."

"You see who did throw it?"

"No," I lied. Why should I get that kid into trouble? I like his spirit.

The soldiers grabbed my two bags of feed. "The army appreciates your support," one of them said. "Now you better leave town, stranger." Then the soldiers left.

I could destroy them all with one fire blast. But I must keep my identity hidden here in the Earth Kingdom. So, I'll leave this village—just as hungry as when I arrived.

"Those soldiers are supposed to protect us from the Fire Nation," the merchant said. "But they're just a bunch of thugs."

Then the kid who threw the egg showed up. "Thanks for not ratting me out," he said. "I'll take you to my house and feed your ostrich-horse for you."

Hmm . . . those thugs did take the feed, and without the ostrich-horse I would be forced to walk in this hot, dry land. Very well. I'll allow him to feed my beast.

The boy led me to his family's farm. There I learned that the boy's name was Lee, and that Lee's older brother, Sen Su, was a soldier fighting in the war.

"Would you like to stay for supper?" Lee's mother asked.

I couldn't stay with this Earth Kingdom family, sit at their table, and accept their food like a friend. I am their enemy. Once the beast is fed, it'd be better for me to leave. "I should be moving on."

"My husband could use some help on the barn," Lee's mother said. "Why don't you two work for a while, and then we'll eat?"

She must have sensed that I didn't want to accept her charity. I would do the work, then eat her food.

As I worked with Lee's father repairing the barn's roof, the boy peppered me with questions. "Where are you from? Where are you going? So how'd you get that scar?"

I wish the boy would just leave me alone.

"Lee, it's not nice to bother people about things they might not want to talk about," his father finally said. "A man's past is his own business."

My past? My past is filled with humiliations at the hands of Azula that now seem like a prelude to what she has done to me in the present.

My mind raced back to my days growing up in the Fire Lord's palace, and to my mother, the only one who ever truly loved me, no matter what. I remember Azula manipulating Mom into forcing me to play with her, then Azula teasing me because her friend Mai liked me. And even worse: Azula always spoke of how Dad would make a better Fire Lord, even though Iroh was older and next in line for the throne.

Dwelling on the past will do me no good. I'd better concentrate on fixing this barn roof.

That night, after the first real meal I'd had in days, I slept soundly in the barn—but not so soundly that I didn't hear Lee sneak in and take my swords. He is a curious boy. I'll let him have his fun.

When I awoke I found Lee outside, swinging the swords wildly. "You're holding them all wrong," I said. If he's going to learn, he should learn correctly. I took the swords from him.

"These are dual swords—two halves of a single weapon. Don't think of them as separate, because they are not." I gave them back to Lee and guided him through some simple exercises. It's nice to be respected, if only by a child. I wonder what he would think if he found out who I really am.

The next day a few Earth Kingdom soldiers came riding onto the farm.

"What do you want?" Lee's father asked.

"Just thought someone ought to tell you— your son's battalion got captured," one of the soldiers said. Then he turned to his comrades. "You boys hear what the Fire Nation did with their last group of Earth Kingdom prisoners?"

"Dressed them up in Fire Nation uniforms and put them on the front lines—unarmed."

I can't believe the Fire Nation would treat prisoners of war that way. It is shameful, lacking all honor.

"What's going to happen to Sen Su?" Lee's mother asked as the soldiers rode away.

The same thing that happens to so many soldiers, whoever they fight for. I remember my cousin Lu Ten, Uncle Iroh's son, and the day my mother told me that he had died during Uncle's attempt to take the Earth Kingdom capital, Ba Sing Se. He was not much older than I was, and suddenly he was gone. Certainly, Uncle has never been the same since.

"I'm going to the front to find Sen Su and bring him back," Lee's father said, snapping my thoughts back to the present.

"When my dad goes, will you stay?" Lee asked me.

"No, I need to move on." I have to go. I can't get involved with this family any deeper than I already am. Still, they did show me kindness. I know—I can repay them with a gift. "Here, I want you to have this."

I handed Lee a pearl-handled dagger that Uncle had sent me from Ba Sing Se, when the war was going well, all those years ago. Before it all went bad for him and he lost his son and his will to fight.

Lee read the inscription that had inspired me when I first saw it. "Never give up without a fight."

As I rode away from the farm I remembered the time my mother told me and Azula that our grandfather, Fire Lord Azulon, had requested an audience with our father—and

all of us.

Once again Azula had made a fool out of me. I stumbled trying to show Grandfather new Firebending moves I'd been practicing, and Azula just laughed.

"I failed," I said as I lay sprawled on the floor at the Fire Lord's feet.

"No," my mother said, rushing to my side as she always did. "I loved watching you. That's who you are, Zuko—someone who keeps fighting even though it's hard."

She is right. Nobody ever knew me like she did. I do keep fighting. It's all I know how to do.

Just like Azula keeps lying to me. It's what she does. She did it on board her ship and she did it when we were kids. She told me that Father was going to severely punish me. That Grandfather was going to discipline Father for suggesting that he, rather than Iroh, become the next Fire Lord. She lies. She always lies.

What's that sound? Someone's approaching. It's a cart carrying Lee's mother. Something's very wrong!

"You have to help. It's Lee. The soldiers came back after my husband left, demanding food. Lee pulled a knife on them. I don't even know where he got it. They told me that if Lee was old enough to fight, he was old enough to join the army. They took him away!"

Even when I try to do the right thing, it goes bad. If I hadn't given him the dagger . . .

"I'll get your son back," I said. It's the least I could do.

I rode into the town square. And I see Lee, tied up next to those thugs. "Let the kid go," I said firmly.

"I told you he'd come!" Lee shouted at his captors.

"Who do you think you are, telling us what to do?" the leader asked threateningly.

Thugs. Punks. They're all the same. I've seem them my whole life. All talk and bluster, with nothing to back it up. Well, it's time some—one put them in their place.

"It doesn't matter who I am. But I know who you are. You're not soldiers, you're bul—lies, freeloaders abusing your power. Mostly over women and kids. You don't want Lee in your army. You're sick cowards messing with a family who's already lost one son to the war."

That got them! Here they come with their feeble attacks. I'll just whip out my swords and put on a few moves, and—there, there they go, running away like the cowards they are. That took even less ef—

"Look out! Behind you!" Lee suddenly shouted.

I turned, just as their leader Earthbended boulders toward me. I couldn't stop them all, and I quickly fell down.

"Get up!" Lee called out. I have to get up. I have to or all is lost . . . lost . . . like the way I lost my mother. My head is spinning, but I can see the past as if it were happening right now, right here.

Mom, slipping into my room at night. I could tell something was wrong.

"Listen, Zuko, my love," she said. She was all dressed up for travel. But where was she going? "Everything I've done, I've done to protect you. Remember this, Zuko, no matter how things may seem to change—never forget who you are!"

I never saw her again. I still have no idea what happened. But I never forgot her last words to me: "Never forget who you are!"

Never forget. Who am I? I am Zuko, Prince of the Fire Nation, and I am finished hiding, lying, and pretending!

I blasted the soldiers with a burst of Fire-bending, then rose to my feet. Everyone's staring at me, including the soldier who's sprawled out on the ground.

"Who are you?" he asked, looking stunned.

No more lying. "My name is Zuko, son of Ursa and Fire Lord Ozai, Prince of the Fire Nation and heir to the throne."

"Liar!" shouted an old man in the crowd. "I've heard of you. You're not a prince, you're an outcast. His own father disowned him!"

No! This was not what I was expecting. These people should respect me. I'm a hero. I just saved them from these thugs. I turned to Lee. He would understand.

"Not a step closer!" Lee's mother shouted at me.

I can see the hatred in her eyes. Then I remembered my dagger, which the soldier had taken. I retrieved it and gave it back to Lee.

32

"It's yours," I said. But he yelled, "No! I hate you!"

There's nothing left to do now but leave. I feel so ashamed of who I am, and so weak and small and filled with dishonor.

I feel so utterly alone.

Chapter 3

I can't go on like this, wandering from town to town with no purpose, no plan. The time has come to take action. I know what I need to do. I must find Azula and defeat her. I am the older child. I am the rightful heir to the throne of the Fire Nation, and I must restore my lost pride and honor. She now stands in my way, and I have to defeat her to put myself back on the right track.

I picked up her trail on board a combination tank and train, capable of traveling anywhere in this rugged nation. The tank—train sends up thick clouds of smoke, and it makes deep rutted tracks in the ground, so it's easy to follow.

After a while, she and her two friends—
Mai and Ty Lee—left the tank-train and
started riding mongoose-dragons. Then they
split up, with Mai and Ty Lee heading in one
direction and Azula riding off in another.

I followed Azula, staying a safe distance
away on my ostrich-horse, but always keep-
ing her in sight. Once she is out of the way
I can resume my search for the Avatar and
complete my quest.

My sister has arrived in a deserted town—or
so it first appeared. To my amazement, there,
sitting in the middle of what must have once
been the town's main street, was the Avatar!

Of course. Azula has been tracking the
Avatar in an attempt to succeed where I have
failed. Well, she has led me to the prize that is
rightfully mine. But first I will take care of her.
Then I will capture the Avatar and bring him
home to Father.

Azula and the Avatar stood, facing off in
the street.

"Do you really want to fight me?" she asked
the Avatar.

It was time to make my appearance. Stepping out from the shadows, I said, "Yes, I really do."

"Zuko!" the Avatar cried.

"I was wondering when you'd show up, Zu-Zu," Azula said.

"Zu-Zu?" the Avatar repeated with a giggle.

She mocks me. That has not changed. But this time I will not let her win. "Back off, Azula. He's mine!"

"I'm not going anywhere," she countered.

I stood ready, shifting my gaze from Azula to the Avatar. Who will make the first move? Should I? Is she more interested in capturing the Avatar, or in battling me and risking his escape?

She's attacking . . . me!

Azula unleashed a Firebending attack that knocked me down. Then she turned her attention to the Avatar. Leaping to my feet, I joined the fight and a three-way battle raged.

Oomph!—she has struck me. I'm going down. No! Not again. She is just too powerful. I'm on the ground, and I can't move. Everything's going dark.

My eyes opened slowly. I see a familiar face. "Uncle!" Why is he here? How did he find me?

"Get up," he said before reaching down and helping me to my feet. Uncle came after me. Even though I walked out on him, he never gave up on me. I wanted to say more to him, but right now we had something more impor—tant to take care of.

Uncle and I faced Azula. Beside us stood the Avatar and his friends.

"Well, look at this," Azula said as we backed her against the wall of an abandoned building. "Enemies and traitors, all working together. I know when I'm beaten. A princess surrenders with honor."

She bowed, but as she raised her head, she suddenly struck, sending a blue Firebending blast right at Uncle!

Noooo!

I unleashed a stream of fire right at Azula. The Avatar and his friends also threw bend—ing attacks at her. When the smoke cleared, Azula was nowhere to be seen.

I can't believe Azula attacked Uncle, but I

shouldn't be surprised. Uncle is a strong man, though, and he was breathing—but he seemed to be in a lot of pain. I cradled his head in my hands to try to keep him comfortable.

Oh, Uncle, how has it come to this? Azula has humiliated me again; and now you, who came to help me, are fighting for your life. Everything's gone bad.

The Avatar and his friends are still here, but I don't care about capturing my prize any—more. I don't care about anything, not if I lose Uncle. "Get away from us!" I shouted. I don't want them staring at us.

"Zuko, I can help," the Waterbending girl said.

I don't want their help. I don't need help, espe—cially not from an enemy. I will not show weak—ness to my enemy. "Leave!" I ordered, and I flung a Firebending blast just above their heads.

As they left, I looked around for some kind of shelter for Uncle. He has to rest. I spotted an abandoned house and carried him in there, where he slept for a long while, trembling and shaking.

When his eyes finally opened, I told him,

"Uncle, you were unconscious. Azula did this to you."

He groaned with pain. I handed him a cup of tea. "I hope I made it the way you like it." My uncle has always taken care of me. It's the least I can do in return.

"So, Uncle, I've been thinking," I said, after awhile. "It's only a matter of time before I run into Azula again. I'm going to need to know more advanced Firebending if I want to stand a chance against her."

 I brace myself for a lecture about family and getting along. "I know what you're going to say—she's my sister and I should be trying to get along with her."

But what Uncle said surprised me!

"No," he said. "She's crazy and she needs to go down. It's time to resume your training."

Uncle seems to be getting stronger. He's going to be okay. And I'm going to continue my train-ing.

He showed me how to create lightning. First he did it, then it was my turn.

Ahhhhh! What happened? No lightning.

Just a big fiery explosion. But why? What's wrong with me? "Why didn't it work? Instead of lightning, it exploded in my face, like every-thing always does!" Again I have failed.

"You will not be able to master lightning until you have dealt with the turmoil inside you."

What is he talking about? "What turmoil?"

"Zuko, you must let go of your feelings of shame if you want your anger to go away."

"Uncle, I don't feel any shame at all. I am as proud as ever."

"True humility is the only antidote to shame."

Humility? Certainly no one knows more about humility than me. "My life has been noth-ing *but* humbling lately," I said. So now what? I can't go home, I can't defeat Azula, and I can't capture the Avatar.

"I have another idea," Uncle said.

He then showed me a way to redirect light-ning.

"Great! I'm ready to try redirecting real lightning," I said after I had practiced a few exercises.

"What, are you crazy? Lightning's very dangerous!"

Why is he showing me this if I don't even get to use it? What's the point? "I thought you taught me this so I could protect myself from lightning."

"Yes, but I'm not going to shoot lightning at you. If you are lucky, you will never have to use this technique at all."

This is a waste of time! If I can't practice the real technique, how will I know it will work when I face Azula? "Well, if you won't help me, I'll find my own lightning!"

I climbed onto my ostrich-horse and gal-

40 loped toward the mountains, in the direction of an approaching storm. I climbed to the top of the mountain as the rain beat down.

I heard thunder in the distance, but it was getting closer. I will find lightning and I will redirect it. Throwing my head back, I thought about all the bad luck that has come my way my whole life, and I shouted up to the heavens, "You've always thrown everything you could at me. Well I can take it, and now I can give it back! Go on, strike me! Strike me with your lightning!"

Why won't the lightning hit me? "Come on,

you've never held back before!" Now when I want danger to find me, it won't. Are the heavens themselves mocking me?

But there was no response. "Ahhhhhh!" I cried out in frustration. I have failed . . . again.

Chapter 4

I give up. I can't spend the rest of my life chasing Azula and losing to her. I've got to move on, find somewhere safe. I returned to Uncle, and, thankfully, he didn't mention my failure with the lightning. We climbed onto the ostrich–horse and rode off.

"Ow–oh–ow–uh." Uncle continued to moan and groan. It was too soon for him to travel. "Maybe we should make camp," I suggested.

"No, please, don't stop just for me. Ow–oh–ow–uh."

Okay, that's it. We have to stop. Why can't Uncle just admit he's in pain? I helped him down from the ostrich-horse and found a place for him to sit. Just as Uncle seemed to be comfortable, we heard the sound of riders approaching.

"What now?" Uncle said, groaning.

A bunch of Fire Nation soldiers riding rhinos burst from the woods and surrounded us.

"Colonel Mongke? What a pleasant surprise," Uncle said.

"You know these guys?"

"Sure, Colonel Mongke and the Rough Rhinos are legendary."

"We're here to apprehend you two fugitives," Colonel Mongke snarled.

"Would you like some tea first?" Uncle asked.

I know Uncle well enough to know that he's not interested in having tea with these men. He's trying to buy himself some time, to prepare for battle. Well, I'm ready too.

"Enough stalling!" Mongke shouted. "Round 'em up!"

Uncle released a wall of fire and I blasted a few others with my own Firebending moves. These soldiers may be legendary, but they were no match for us! Within a few moments we were back on the ostrich-horse making our escape.

"It's nice to see old friends," Uncle said.

Always making jokes, Uncle. Some things never change. "Too bad you don't have any old friends who don't want to attack you."

"Hmm . . . old friends that don't want to attack me?"

Uh-oh, what's he thinking now? What idea did I just give him? Whatever it is, I'm sure I'll find out soon enough.

Uncle led us to a rundown old dive called the Misty Palms Oasis Cantina. "You think we're going to find someone to help us in this place? These people just look like filthy wanderers."

"So do we," Uncle said. "Ah, this is inter-esting. I think I've found our friend."

He was staring at an old man sitting at a Pai Sho table. "You brought us here to gamble on Pai Sho?" I asked.

"I don't think this is a gamble," he replied, walking over to the man.

"May I have this game?" Uncle asked. The

man nodded, then Uncle made the first move.

"I see you favor the white lotus gambit," the old man said. "Not many still cling to the ancient ways."

"Those who do can always find a friend," Uncle answered—a little mysteriously, I thought.

They placed pieces on the board quickly. It didn't even look like they were playing Pai Sho. It looked more like they were making some kind of picture with the pieces. After a while they stopped. Now what was the old man going to do?

"Welcome, brother," he said. "The White Lotus opens wide to those who know her secrets."

First crazy Pai Sho patterns, now strange talk. What are we even doing here? "What are you old gas bags talking about?" I asked.

"I always tried to tell you that Pai Sho is more than just a game," Uncle said.

Well, what does that mean? Before I had the chance to ask more questions, two men came toward us.

"It's over!" the taller man shouted. "You two

fugitives are coming with me!"

We've got to get out. But Uncle's new friend jumped to his feet and pointed at us. "I knew it!" he shouted. "You two are wanted criminals with a giant bounty on your heads!"

I thought Uncle had gotten the guy on our side. "You said he would help!" I whispered to Uncle.

"He is," Uncle whispered back. "Just watch."

The old man turned to the ones who had approached us. "You think you're going to col—

lect all that gold?" he yelled.

Now he had everyone in the place standing and staring at us. The tall man moved toward us, but a crowd started forming around him! Soon a huge brawl broke out, and Uncle's friend signaled for us to slip out the side door. I finally got it. By shouting about gold the old guy set off the brawl as a distraction. We had to follow him and get out of here before anyone realized that we were gone.

But I still have no idea who this guy really is. Can we trust him? He led us to a flower shop, looking back over his shoulder the whole way.

"It is an honor to welcome such a high rank-ing member of the Order of the White Lotus," the man said when we were inside and he had once again checked to make sure that we hadn't been followed.

The Order of the White Lotus? More mysterious talk. Why are we here? "Now that you've played Pai Sho, are you going to do some flower arranging, or is someone in this secret club going to offer some real help?" I asked again.

"You must forgive my nephew," Uncle told the man. "He is not an initiate and has little appreciation for the cryptic arts."

We reached a door at the back of the shop. A small panel in the door slid open.

"Who knocks at the garden gate?" asked a man behind the door.

"One who has eaten the fruit and tasted its mysteries," Uncle replied.

More crazy talk, but the door did open. At least maybe someone in there can help and—WHAM! Uncle and the man just went in and slammed the door in my face! What am I, invisible? A small panel opened and my uncle's face peeked through.

"I'm afraid it's members only," he said. "Wait out here."

Oh, great. So I can't even see what's going on in this secret club of theirs. I waited . . . and waited . . . and waited. What's taking so long? What are they doing in there?

I dozed off for a while before they finally came out. "What's going on? Is the club meet—ing over?" I asked.

"Everything is taken care of," Uncle said. "We're heading to Ba Sing Se."

48

"Ba Sing Se? Why would we go to the Earth Kingdom capital?"

"The city is filled with refugees," Uncle's new friend said. "No one will notice two more."

"We can hide in plain sight there," Uncle explained. "And it's the safest place in the world from the Fire Nation. Even I couldn't break through to the city."

So we really are giving up, going to hide in the Earth Kingdom capital where Azula can't find us. We're not going home. I'm not going to fight my sister, capture the Avatar, or reclaim my honor. I'm going to spend the rest of my life as a fugitive, a refugee, hiding from the world. Mostly hiding from myself. I never thought it would end like this, but I really don't have other choices right now.

Suddenly a man rushed into the room carry—ing some papers. He seemed to be in a panic. "I have the passports for our two guests, but there are two men out on the street looking for them," he said.

I peered out the front window of the shop.

It was the two men from the cantina. They were showing a wanted poster to everyone on the street. What do we do now? Run? Hide? Stay and fight?

Uncle's friend pointed to two vases that were large enough to hide in. We quickly slipped into the huge clay pots and Uncle's friend placed some soil and flowers over our heads.

I squatted in the dark, hiding under the dirt and flowers, and trying to make out what was happening. I could feel that we were moving in some kind of cart. I could hear the squeaking wheels of the cart rolling us from the shop.

Then I heard the two men from the

cantina yelling at Uncle's friend, but their voices sounded far away. I guessed we were moving away from the shop, toward our new life in Ba Sing Se.

Chapter 5

We made our way to the boat dock, then, using our fake passports, boarded the ferry to Ba Sing Se.

"Who would have thought that after all these years I'd return to the scene of my greatest military disgrace . . . as a tourist!" Uncle said, putting on a silly hat and laughing.

How can he joke about our utter defeat? Here we are, a great general and a prince, running away to hide in the stronghold of our enemy. At this point, I am doubtful that we'll ever see our home again. We'll be prisoners within a walled city, afraid to venture out for fear of encountering Azula. What exactly is there to joke about? I find no humor in shame. "Look around, Uncle. We're not tourists, we're refugees."

I slurped down a sip of the slop they fed us and quickly spat it overboard. "Ugh. I'm sick of eating rotten food, sleeping in the dirt. I'm tired of living like this!"

"Aren't we all?" said a soft voice from behind me.

I turned to see three guys—refugees, judging by their looks.

"My name's Jet," one of them said. "And these are my freedom fighters, Smellerbee and Longshot.

"Hey," Smellerbee said.

Longshot just nodded.

"Hello," I said cautiously. Freedom fighters? What do these guys want from me?

"Here's the deal," Jet began. "I hear the captain's eating like a king while us refugees have to feed off the scraps. Doesn't seem fair, does it?" He stared at me as he asked, "You want to help us liberate some food?"

I like the sound of that. I'm ready to eat like

a king. And I'm sure Uncle is, too. "I'm in," I replied, tossing the bowl of swill overboard.

That night, Jet, Smellerbee, and I made our way up to the captain's quarters. Through the window I saw a huge amount of food spread out on a big table. It looked like someone was about to have a feast. And that someone is me.

Jet popped open the lock with his sword. He and I slipped in while Smellerbee stood guard. I cut down some roast ducks, then gathered up boxes of food with my swords, stacking and tying them in one swift motion. Just like old times—only without the blue mask.

"Guards coming!" Smellerbee called out.

That was our signal to leave. We grabbed a few more items, then ducked back out and headed down to the lower deck with our feast. Uncle, Smellerbee, Longshot, and I dug into the delicious food while Jet handed some out to the other refugees.

I like this guy. He has an idea, makes a plan, and takes action. And because of that, we refugees have the food we deserve.

"From what I heard, people eat like this

every night in Ba Sing Se," Jet said, sitting down and joining us. "I can't wait to set my eyes on that giant wall."

"It's a magnificent sight," Uncle said.

"So you've been there before?" Jet asked.

I stiffened slightly, not sure how Uncle was going to handle this. He can't let on that we're Fire Nation.

"Once," he replied. "When I was a . . . different man."

Okay, I hope Jet doesn't ask Uncle to elaborate. And he didn't. Jet nodded as if he understood. "I've done some things in my past that I'm not proud of. But that's why I'm going to Ba Sing Se—for a new beginning, a second chance."

"That's very noble of you," Uncle said. Then he looked right at me as he added, "I believe people can change their lives if they want to. I believe in second chances."

Is that what this is about? A second chance rather than a failure? A chance to leave my old life behind once and for all? A chance to start over in a place where no one knows me? Forget who I am . . . who I was? Maybe this is an opportunity rather than a defeat. I'm just not sure.

The following morning as I stood at the ferry's railing, watching the ship approach the great wall of Ba Sing Se, Jet stepped up beside me.

"You know, as soon as I saw your scar, I knew exactly who you were," he said.

What—he knows I'm Fire Nation? That I'm a prince in exile? How can he?

"You're an outcast, like me," Jet continued.

Oh, okay. He has no idea. I was relieved.

55

"And us outcasts have to stick together. We have to watch each other's backs. Because no one else will."

I understood what he was telling me. "I've realized lately that being on your own isn't always the best path," I replied. Maybe I've met another "outcast" who thinks like I do. Maybe things in Ba Sing Se won't be so bad after all. Maybe.

We arrived at Ba Sing Se's outer wall and, with the fake passports Uncle's friends at the White Lotus club had given us, easily passed through the processing center.

Now that we were in, we waited for the monorail to take us into the city itself so we could start our new lives. I'm still not sure what that means, but I can't stop thinking about Uncle speaking of a second chance.

Jet came over. "So, you guys got plans once you're in the city?" he asked.

Before I could reply, a tea salesman came by. "Get your hot tea here! Finest tea in Ba Sing Se."

"Ohh!" Uncle cried. "Jasmine, please!" But he took one sip and spat it out. "Ugh. *Coldest* tea in Ba Sing Se is more like it!"

56

As Uncle scowled and stared at his cold cup of tea, I got up and walked away, hoping to avoid Jet's questions. But he kept after me.

"You and I have a much better chance of making it in the city if we stick together," Jet said. "You want to join my freedom fighters?"

I'm not surprised that Jet asked me to join his gang. It might be a good idea, part of my second chance. They can help me create my new destiny away from the Fire Nation, and forge a new path. But is that what I really want to be doing? I don't know what I want. Can I really change from being a Fire Nation prince to being a commoner, a refugee? Deep down inside I know that I cannot change or deny who I really am. And sooner or later Jet's going to realize that I am Fire Nation, that I am his enemy. No, I think for now, at least, I must remain on my own.

"Thanks," I replied. "But I don't think you want me in your gang."

He wouldn't let me off the hook, though. "Come on," he said. "We made a great team looting that captain's food. Think of all the good we could do for these refugees."

Refugees that are here and homeless because of my people—because of my father. "I said no."

"Have it your way," Jet said. I can tell he's annoyed.

I turned and walked back toward Uncle. When I saw what was in his hand, I froze for a second. What was he thinking? He's risking exposing us as Firebenders just to make his tea hot! I hoped that Jet didn't see the steam rising from the cup, but I could tell it was too late. Jet stared suspiciously at us before walking away quickly.

"For a wise old man," I whispered. "That was a pretty stupid move."

Uncle didn't respond and I didn't press the issue. We had more important things to think about right now. The monorail finally came. We got on and took our seats. So many people going to the city, all hoping for a new life. All except me. The closer I now get to my chance for a new life, the more I miss the old one. However much I try to deny it, I am still a prince in exile, hiding in the stronghold of my enemy.

58

Arriving in the city center we found an apartment, then headed out to the marketplace. Uncle picked up a huge bouquet of flowers. "I just want our new place to look nice," he said to me.

What is he talking about? He's acting like everything is fine. Like being here is a good thing. It's not. "This city is a prison. I don't want to make a life here."

"Life happens wherever you are, whether

you make it or not."

More lectures. More philosophy. I don't want to hear it.

"Now come on," Uncle continued. "I found us some jobs and we start this afternoon."

Jobs! He really is trying to make a life here. The only job I want is as Prince of the Fire Nation, and then someday as Fire Lord. But I guess that's not going to happen, is it?

We came to a small tea shop and Uncle stepped inside. Of course. He got us jobs in a tea shop. What else would he do? So it comes to this—serving tea to rich people and Earth Kingdom soldiers. My new life. I hate it already.

Pao, the owner of the shop, handed us aprons. I slipped mine on. Ugh, this is so humiliating!

"Well, you certainly look like official tea servers," Pao said. "How do you feel?"

"Ridiculous," I muttered, not caring if he heard me.

Uncle sipped some tea. "Ugh! This tea is nothing more than hot leaf juice!"

"Uncle, that's what all tea is," I pointed out.

"How could a member of my own family say something so horrible?" Uncle said. Then he looked around the shop. "We'll have to make some major changes around here."

Sure. Whatever you want, Uncle. I really don't care.

That evening we returned to our apartment. I was actually exhausted from standing on my feet, carrying trays of tea to people all day. I stretched out on the couch to rest.

"Would you like a pot of tea?" Uncle asked.

"We've been working in a tea shop all day," I replied. "I'm sick of tea."

"Sick of tea?" Uncle said. "That's like being sick of breathing."

For you maybe, Uncle. But not me. I am sick of everything, of my whole life. I just want to rest.

🔶 🔶 🔶

And so my life goes. Day in and day out. Wake up. Go to work. Serve tea. Come home. Sleep. Do the same thing tomorrow. This city feels more and more like a prison each day.

One evening we were in the shop serving

tea to a group of Earth Kingdom soldiers.

"This is the best tea in the city," one soldier said.

Uncle beamed. Naturally. "The secret ingredient is love," he said.

"I think you're due for a raise," Pao told us.

That's nice. At least we'll have a bit more—

Suddenly Jet burst through the shop's front door, flashing his two hook-swords.

What's he doing here? What's he trying to do? He's pointing at us.

"These two men are Firebenders!" he shouted.

I knew it! I knew he saw Uncle heat his tea that day at the monorail station. A foolish move that could now cost us everything.

Jet turned to the soldiers. "I know they're Firebenders. I saw the old man heating his tea!"

"He works in a tea shop," one of the soldiers replied, looking at Jet like he was crazy.

Stay calm now. Ride this out. The soldiers have no reason to believe him. They like Uncle. They love his tea. All of this can work in our favor. Just relax, Zuko.

"He's a Firebender, I'm telling you!" Jet shouted again.

The soldiers stood up slowly. "Drop your swords, boy. Nice and easy."

Jet ignored them and rushed toward Uncle. "You'll have to defend yourself. Then everyone will know what you can do. Go ahead. Show them what you can do."

I can stop him—without Firebending! I stepped forward and snatched a pair of swords from the soldiers. "You want a show, I'll give you a show!"

I swung the blade and Jet met my attack with a swift movement of his hook–swords. The battle was on. Everyone jumped out of the way as we fought, leaping and slashing, hurling over tables and crashing into teapots.

Jet's good . . . but I'm better!

He lunged forward, slamming into me, sending us both crashing through the front door. We tumbled out onto the street. Uncle, Pao, and the soldiers followed, and a crowd gathered as our battle raged on.

"You must be getting tired of using these

swords," Jet taunted me. "Why don't you go ahead and Firebend at me?"

I swiped at him again, but he blocked the blow and countered with an attack of his own.

"Please, son, you're confused!" Uncle shouted. "You don't know what you're doing!"

Our swords locked, then his eyes fixed firmly on mine. "Bet you wish he'd help you out with a little fire blast right now," Jet snarled.

I shoved him back. "You're the one who needs help." My next swipe nearly caught him, but he ducked and rolled away.

"You see that?" he shouted, trying to appeal to the huge crowd of Earth Kingdom citizens who continued to gather. "The Fire Nation is trying to silence me! It'll never happen!" Then he lunged forward again.

Jet showed no sign of letting up, and I was certainly not going to give any ground. It's good to know that these weeks working in the tea shop haven't dulled my fighting skills.

Suddenly a group of Earth Kingdom soldiers burst through the crowd. With them were agents of the Dai Li, the king's personal guards. I had heard people talk about them, about how even the soldiers feared them.

"Drop your weapons!" a Dai Li agent shouted.

"Arrest them!" Jet yelled back. "They're Firebenders!"

Uncle stepped forward. "This poor boy is confused. We're simple refugees."

Then Pao pointed at Jet. "This young man wrecked my tea shop and assaulted my employees!"

One of the soldiers who had been in the shop stepped forward. "It's true, sir. We saw the whole thing. This crazy kid attacked the finest tea-maker in the city."

Who will they believe?

The Dai Li agents grabbed Jet. "Come with us, son."

"You don't understand! They're Fire Nation!" Jet cried, as several more Dai Li agents used Earthbending to slap rock hand-cuffs onto Jet and haul him away. "You have to believe me!"

They tossed Jet into the back of their truck, slammed the door, and drove away.

Our secret is still safe—for now.

Chapter 6

There's that same girl. She comes into the tea shop every day. And she's always staring at me. She must suspect that I'm Fire Nation. What other explanation could there be?

"Uncle, we have a problem. Don't look now, but there is a girl at the corner table. She knows we're Fire Nation."

"I've seen that girl in here a lot," Uncle replied. "Seems she has quite a little crush on you."

"What?" A crush? What is he talking about? I'm sure she's a spy and—

"Thank you for the tea. What's your name?"

It's the girl. She's talking to me! Think fast, Zuko. I have to use the name on my fake passport. "My name's Lee. My uncle and I just moved here."

"Hi, Lee. My name's Jin. I was wondering if you would like to go out sometime."

"He'd love to," Uncle said, answering before I even had a chance to think.

"Great!" Jin said. "I'll meet you in front of the shop at sundown."

Oh, great! Now Uncle's pushing me into a . . . a date! Thanks a lot. I don't want to go on a date. I don't know what to talk about. Everything I can say would just be a lie anyway. I certainly can't tell this girl the truth about who I am. Why did Uncle do that? I really don't want to go.

But when the shop closed, Jin was outside waiting for me. She took my arm and we started walking through the city. We stopped at a restaurant and ordered some food.

"So, how do you like the city so far?" Jin asked.

"It's okay." What am I supposed to say?

"What do you do for fun?"

"Nothing." Fun. I'm not a child anymore. I don't have time for fun. This really is not going well.

Then the waiter came over. At least that stops me from having to talk for a few seconds. "Excuse me, sir. Would you and your girlfriend care for dessert?"

Girlfriend! What is he talking about? I just met this girl. I don't even want to be here! "She is not my girlfriend!" I snapped.

Great. Now I'm making a scene. She prob—ably hates me for shouting that out. When is this evening going to be over?

"So, Lee, where were you and your uncle living before you came here?"

How do I answer that one? Keep it vague. "Um, well, we've been traveling all around for a long time."

"Oh, why were you traveling so much?"

Think of a good lie. Something she'll believe so she'll stop asking all these questions. "We were . . . part of a traveling circus." Dumb, Zuko. Really dumb.

"Really? What did you do? Wait. Let me guess . . . you juggled."

Sure. That's as good a lie as any. "Yes. I juggled." Now can I go home?

"I've always wanted to learn how to juggle. Can you show me something?"

She's handing me three clay pots. I can't juggle. I'm just going to break this stuff. I tossed the pots into the air and tried to catch them, but they crashed down all around me, smashing to bits. "I haven't practiced for a while." She's going to know I'm lying.

"It's all right," Jin said, smiling.

She was nice enough not to give me a hard time. "Hey, I want to show you one of my favorite places in the city," she said. "I'm so excited for you to see the Firelight Fountain. The lamps make the water sparkle and reflect in the pool in the most beautiful way."

We came to a large fountain. The water was shooting into the air and splashing down into a large pool, but the lamps all around it were dark.

"I can't believe it!" Jin cried. "The lamps aren't lit."

She looked so disappointed. She really wanted to show me this and now the evening

is turning out badly for her. I shouldn't do this . . .
but she's been so nice to me. It'll be okay if
she doesn't see me do it. "Close your eyes and
don't peek."

When Jin's hands were securely covering
her eyes, I performed a simple Firebending
move, sending a flame from lamp to lamp until
they were all lit. She is right. The water does
sparkle, and it is beautiful. It also feels so good
to Firebend again, even this little bit. "Okay,
now you can look."

Jin opened her eyes and her face lit up
almost as brightly as the fountain lamps. "Oh,
wow! What happened? How did they light?
What did you—" She stopped asking questions and her smile just got bigger and bigger.

She was so sweet I'm sure that she didn't
even think that I might be a Firebender. I did
do the right thing. She looked so happy. That
kind of makes me feel happy, too. She leaned
in to kiss me. I don't know if I should kiss her.
I—wait, I almost forgot. "I brought you something," I said, holding up a coupon between us.
"It's a coupon for a free cup of tea."

That made her smile some more.

"Lee, this is so sweet."

"Don't thank me. It was my uncle's idea. He thinks you are our most valuable customer."

"I have something for you, too," she said. "Now it's your turn to close your eyes."

Okay, my eyes are closed. What's she going to do? I wonder if—oh, she is, she's kissing me. I can't let her do that. I can't get involved with this girl. Everything she thinks she knows about me is a lie. And that's all it could ever be. I could never let her know the truth. I have to pull away.

"What's wrong?" Jin asked.

Now I've made her feel bad. I really didn't want to do that. "It's complicated." *I can't stay here with her anymore.* "I have to go."

I hurried back to the apartment.

"How was your night, Prince Zuko?" Uncle asked when I walked in.

I don't want to talk about it. I stepped into my room and slammed the door shut. *I don't know. I actually like this girl. But I can't let this develop into anything. It would be based on lies, and I can't have that. Still, I enjoyed doing something that made someone else happy. And tonight I felt* happy for a few minutes. I can't remember the last time I felt this way. I opened my door and stuck out my head.

"It was nice," I said. It really had been.

A few days later some wealthy merchants came into the tea shop and offered Uncle his own tea shop. "I'll provide you with a new apartment in the Upper Ring," one of the merchants said. "And your new tea shop is yours to do with as you please—complete creative freedom."

"Did you hear that, Nephew?" Uncle said excitedly. "This man wants to give us our own tea shop in the Upper Ring of the city!"

"That's right, young man, your life is about to change for the better," the merchant said to me.

"I'll try to contain my joy," I replied.

I have to step outside. So now we dig ourselves deeper into this city. A new shop, a new apartment in the fancy section of town. More responsibilities. More of a permanent life here. More lies. I don't want to do this anymore!

Just then a piece of paper drifted down

from the sky. It was a drawing of the Avatar's bison. Then another flyer fell. They were falling all over.

The Avatar must have made these. He has lost his bison and is searching for it here in Ba Sing Se. So the Avatar is also here, in the city, close at hand. This is the chance I've been waiting for, the chance to leave all this behind and seize my true destiny.

Perhaps that merchant is right, after all. Maybe my life *is* about to change for the better.

When I got home I found Uncle packing his things. He was smiling, happy. Everything was going right for him. "So I was thinking about names for my new tea shop. How about 'The Jasmine Dragon'?"

"The Avatar is here in Ba Sing Se and he's lost his bison." I showed Uncle the flyer.

"We have a chance for a new life here," Uncle said. Exactly what I thought he would say. "If you start stirring up trouble we could lose all the good things that are happening for us."

Nothing good has happened to me. "Good

things are happening for *you*," I told Uncle. "Have you ever thought that I want more from my life than a nice apartment and a job serving tea?" I can try to fool myself, but I am who I am, and nothing will ever change that.

"There's nothing wrong with a life of peace and prosperity. I suggest you think about what it is that you want from your life . . . and why."

"I want my destiny."

"What that means is up to you."

Up to me? He's talking like I have a choice as to what my destiny is. Do I? How can I? I am Prince Zuko, next in line to be Fire Lord. I have always known what that meant. And now, once again, my destiny is within my grasp.

But first I need to enlist the services of an old friend.

Disguised as the Blue Spirit, I ambushed a Dai Li agent and forced him to tell me where the bison was being held. It turned out that he's being kept in a cell in the Dai Li's secret hide-out under a lake called Lake Laogai. I made my way there and quickly found the cell.

Stepping inside, I brandished my swords,

and the great furry beast growled at me.

"Expecting someone else?" I asked. At last, I'm one step away from the Avatar. "You're mine now."

Before I could take my next step, the door behind me slid open. I prepared to launch a surprise attack on my opponent. But I was the one who was surprised. "Uncle?"

"So, the Blue Spirit. I wonder who could be behind that mask?" he asked, although he knew the answer.

I tossed my mask and swords to the ground.
"What are you doing here?"

"I was just about to ask you the same thing," Uncle replied. "What do you plan to do now that you've found the Avatar's bison? Keep it locked in our new apartment? Should I go put on a pot of tea for him?"

"First I have to get it out of here."

"And then what!" Uncle shouted at me. I had never seem him this furious. "You never think these things through!"

"I know my own destiny, Uncle." I will not let him talk me out of this. I will not let him doom me to a life of making tea.

"Is it your own destiny? Or is it a destiny someone else has tried to force on you?"

I won't listen to his double-talk. He's just trying to confuse me. "Stop it, Uncle! I have to do this!"

"I'm begging you, Prince Zuko. It's time for you to look inward, and begin asking yourself the big questions. Who are you? What do you want!"

Can he be right? Can my desire to fulfill my role as prince, to capture the Avatar, to restore my honor—even to become Fire Lord—all be someone else's dream? What I *think* I'm supposed to do rather than what *I* want? I don't know. I'm not sure of anything right now.

What I do know is that Uncle is right about the Avatar's bison. What would I do with it? Where would I keep it? There are no easy answers.

I looked over at the creature one more time. It is trapped. I understand how that feels. And it is not a good feeling.

I released the bison, then Uncle and I headed for home.

Chapter 7

76 As we entered our apartment, I felt dizzy and light-headed. Something was wrong with me.

"You did the right thing, letting the Avatar's bison go free," Uncle said.

"I don't feel well." The room is spinning. Everything's getting blurry . . . going dark . . . just darkness . . .

"Zuko!"

I barely heard Uncle shout as the floor came rushing up toward me and I passed out.

As I slowly woke up, it felt like I was moving through a thick fog. My head was pounding and my eyes felt like they were on fire. Every part of my body hurts.

"You're burning up," Uncle said. I was stretched out on a sleeping roll on the floor under heavy blankets. "You have an intense fever." Uncle leaned over me, wiping my face with a wet cloth. "This will cool you down."

"So thirsty." I've never felt more parched, like my throat was shriveling up.

"I'll get you some clean water to drink. Stay under the blankets and sweat this out."

I drank a ladleful of cool water, then grabbed the whole bucket and gulped it down. I felt as if I could drink an entire lake. I put my head down and drifted back into a deep sleep. And as I slept, I had a strange, disturbing dream.

I am Fire Lord Zuko. All is as it should be. I sit upon my throne, flames dancing all around me, as my army awaits my orders. A blue dragon slithers alongside me on my right, while a red dragon raises its scaly head to my left.

"It's getting late," hissed the blue dragon. "Are you planning to retire soon, my Lord?"

"I'm not tired."

"Relax, Fire Lord Zuko," the blue dragon cooed. "Just let go. Give in to it. Shut your eyes for a while."

That sounds good. It makes sense. Perhaps I should get some rest. Being Fire Lord is a tiring responsibility.

"No, Fire Lord Zuko!" cried the red dragon. "Do not listen to the blue dragon. You should get out of here. Right now."

Hmm . . . which dragon is right? What should I do? Stay or go?

"Go! Before it's too late!" shouted the red dragon.

My palace is crumbling all around me. My soldiers are vanishing before my eyes. Now the blue dragon moves toward me, emerging from the darkness.

"Sleep," the blue dragon said. "Just like Mother!"

The blue dragon's mouth is open wide and . . . no, it can't be . . . Mother is trapped inside the blue dragon.

"Zuko!" Mother cried. "Help me!"

Now I'm being swallowed up by my own

throne. It's all wrong. It's all falling apart. Going bad! Nooo!

It took me a few minutes to absorb my sur—roundings. Where am I? Oh, I was still in bed, in the apartment in Ba Sing Se. I realized that I was still sick. And I was not the Fire Lord after all. I had had a nightmare.

Uncle was preparing tea for me. "You should know this is not a natural sickness," he said, lifting a steaming cup to my lips. "But that shouldn't stop you from enjoying tea."

"What's happening?"

"Your critical decision—what you did beneath that lake—was in such conflict with your image of yourself that you are now at war within your own mind and body," Uncle explained.

"What does that mean?"

"You are going through a metamorphosis, my nephew. It will not be a pleasant experi—ence. But when you come out of it, you will be the beautiful prince you were always meant to be."

A conflict? Between the part of me that

knew it was right to set the bison free, and the way I've always pictured myself, as a ruthless soldier of the Fire Nation? I do feel a battle raging within my mind and body. But which part of me will win?

I fell back to sleep. When I finally woke up, I slipped from my bed and walked past Uncle. He was asleep, and I didn't want to wake him. He had been up for days taking care of me.

I went to the bathroom and splashed water on my face. I paused for a moment, finding something unfamiliar. The skin where my scar is feels soft and smooth again, like before the scar was there.

I looked into the mirror.

My scar was gone! How could that be? And what's that on my head? A tattoo! The Avatar's arrow tattoo! What have I become? Noooo . . .

I bolted upright in bed. A dream. That whole thing was just a dream. I was not in the bathroom. I was in bed.

I ran my hand over my face. My scar was still there.

What could that dream mean? Am I moving toward the part of me that helped the Avatar? Is the Fire Nation losing the battle within me? I wish I knew what it all meant.

Chapter 8

82 The sounds of birds chirping drifted through my open window, easing me gently from sleep. I woke up in my comfortable bed, in my own room, in our new apartment. Somehow the sun seemed brighter here. And all trace of my fever is gone. I feel fantastic. My mind feels sharp and clear. No conflict, no battle—just hungry!

I joined Uncle in our new spacious kitchen. Something smelled wonderful! "What's that smell?"

"It's jook. I'm sure you wouldn't like it."

I leaned over the pot of bubbling cereal.

"Actually, it smells delicious. I'd love a bowl, Uncle."

"Now that your fever is gone, you seem different somehow," Uncle said, smiling and handing me the bowl.

I feel different. I feel happy, at peace for the first time in years. "It's a new day," I said. "We've got a new apartment, new furniture, and today's the grand opening of your new tea shop. Things are looking up, Uncle."

It all seems so simple now, I can't even remember why I ever felt conflicted. We have a chance for a good life here, a new start. And I'm going to make the most of it.

We stood in front of Uncle's new tea shop, The Jasmine Dragon. It was big and beautiful, and packed with customers. I feel so proud of him. This is truly a special day.

"Who thought when we came to this city as refugees that I'd end up owning my own tea shop?" Uncle said as he gazed out at the crowd. "Follow your passion, Zuko, and life will reward you."

As usual, he was right. "Congratulations, Uncle."

"I'm very thankful."

"You deserve it. The Jasmine Dragon will be the best tea shop in the city."

"No. I'm thankful because you decided to share this special day with me. It means more than you know."

No one has ever been kinder to me or stuck with me no matter what. I gave Uncle a big hug. "Now let's make these people some tea!"

It's day one of my new life, and I can't imagine anywhere else I'd rather be.

  At the end of our first day, Uncle was sweeping up before we headed home when a messenger arrived.

"A message from the royal palace," the messenger said, handing him a scroll. Then he turned and left.

"I—I can't believe it," Uncle said when he read the scroll. "Great news! We've been invited to serve tea . . . to the Earth King!"

It was an honor. Uncle's reputation has spread quickly throughout the city. Things just continue to get better and better.

As we approached the Earth King's palace my excitement grew. I couldn't believe I was really going to serve tea to the Earth King.

"Many times I imagined myself here, at the threshold of the palace," Uncle said. "But I always thought I would be here as a conqueror, not as the king's personal guest, here to serve him tea. Destiny is a funny thing."

"It sure is, Uncle." Destiny. For so long I was certain I knew what my destiny would be. Now I realize that Uncle is right. Destiny is what you make it, and I have made the right choice.

We entered the palace tea room and set up for a royal tea ceremony. And then we waited, and waited. "What's taking so long?" I asked Uncle.

"Maybe the Earth King overslept?" Uncle whispered.

Suddenly about fifteen Dai Li agents came into the room. This seemed strange. Why would they be here for a tea ceremony? "Something's not right," I said.

Then someone else stepped into the room. "It's tea time," said an all—too—familiar voice.

"Azula!" No! She's here, dressed in the uniform of the Dai Li. I stood and readied myself for battle. All of my instincts kicked in, along with my lifelong feeling of dread at the sight of my sister.

"Have you met the Dai Li?" Azula asked. "They're Earthbenders, but they have a killer instinct that's so Firebender. I just love it."

What I fool I was! This was all a trap—the whole thing, the invitation, the new shop. Nothing ever changes. Once again Azula taunts me. We're completely surrounded. I  don't see a way out, but Uncle does.

86

"Did I ever tell you how I got the nickname 'The Dragon of the West'?" Uncle asked.

What's he doing?

"I'm not interested in a lengthy anecdote, Uncle," Azula replied.

"It's more of a demonstration, really."

Uncle took a sip of hot tea. Then I knew what he was going to do, and I was ready. I ducked just as Uncle attacked using his trademark bending technique—shooting fire from his mouth—and spraying it in a circle at all the Dai Li.

I bolted from the tea room, exploding through the wall, then dashed down a hallway. Uncle followed close behind, spraying fire back into the room before he joined me in a dead run.

Reaching the far wall, Uncle blasted a hole in it, then leaped to the ground below, crashing into a hedge. I reached the hole and looked down. Behind me the Dai Li approached.

"Come on!" Uncle shouted from below. "You'll be fine!"

Do I jump and once again run with Uncle as a fugitive, or do I turn and fight Azula? Should I settle this—and so much else—right here, right now?

"No. I'm tired of running," I said. "It's time I faced Azula." I can never be truly free to be what I choose to be until I confront her.

I turned and headed back down the hall. There she stood with the Dai Li agents behind her.

"You're so dramatic," she said. "What, are you going to challenge me to an agni kai?"

An agni kai—a fire duel, the challenge in which Father gave me this scar. If that's what it takes I will gladly duel Azula. "Yes. I challenge you."

"No thanks," she said, shrugging.

I don't care what she says. We are going to have this out right now! I unleashed a fire blast right at Azula, but the Dai Li stepped in front of her and used Earthbending to raise a section of the stone floor, stopping my fire.

Then they flung hands of stone at me. Controlled by Earthbending, the flying rock hands grabbed my arms and legs. I was trapped. And Azula didn't even have to put up a fight!

The Dai Li dragged me down a hallway, then tossed me down a tunnel. I bounced off rough rock walls before landing in some kind of underground prison. And there was someone else in it.

"Zuko!"

I knew that voice. She stepped into the light. It was Katara, the Waterbender who travels with the Avatar.

I had nothing to say to her, so I crawled to a corner and turned my face to the wall.

How could everything have gone so wrong so fast? One minute I was about to serve tea to the Earth King, happy in my new life and in the destiny I chose for myself. The next moment

Azula showed up to ruin everything—as she has done many times before. How could I not have known that my happiness would be short-lived? Maybe this is my destiny: to be tortured by my younger sister for the rest of my life.

Apparently Katara did not care that I did not want to talk. She came over and immediately launched into a verbal assault. "Why did they throw you in here? As a trap to catch Aang? You're a terrible person, you know that? Following us, hunting the Avatar. Trying to capture the world's last hope for peace. But what do you care? You're the Fire Lord's son. Spreading war and violence and hatred is in your blood!"

"You don't know what you're talking about," I said.

"I don't? How dare you. You have no idea what this war has put me through—me personally. The Fire Nation took my mother away from me."

How can I explain to her that I'm as much a victim of this war as she is? "I'm sorry," I said. "That's something we have in common."

That stopped Katara's tirade. We sat in

silence for a long while, then Katara apologized. "I'm sorry I yelled at you before."

"It doesn't matter."

"It's just that for so long now, whenever I would imagine the face of the enemy, it was your face."

"My face." So she mocks me because I'm scarred. "I see." I touched my scar. It feels as if that's all she can see when she looks at me.

"No, that's not what I meant."

"It's okay. I used to think this scar marked me. The mark of the banished prince, cursed to chase the Avatar forever. But lately, I've realized I'm free to determine my own destiny, even if I'll never be free of my mark."

"Maybe you could be free of it," Katara said. "I have healing abilities."

What is she talking about? "It's a scar. It can't be healed." Then she pulled out a vial.

"This is water from the spirit oasis at the North Pole. It has special properties. I've been saving it for something important. I don't know if it would work, but . . ."

She gently touched my scar.

THOOM! Suddenly a wall of the cell

exploded. There stood my uncle—with the Avatar! "Uncle, I don't understand," I said. "What are you doing with the Avatar?"

"Saving you, that's what," the Avatar said.

Well, that's what I don't need right now: to be taunted by the Avatar. I will fight him right here and—

"Prince Zuko!" Uncle shouted, grabbing me and holding me back. "It's time we talked."

Katara and the Avatar ran off to help their friends. I looked up at Uncle. "Why?"

"You are not the man you used to be, Zuko. You are stronger and wiser and freer than you have ever been. And now you have come to the crossroads of your destiny. It's time for you to choose. Time for you to choose good!"

He's right. I am free to choose and I do choose—

At that moment crystal spikes exploded from the ground all around us. Azula and two Dai Li agents slid down the rock tunnel and stopped right beside me.

"I expected this kind of treachery from Uncle, but Prince Zuko . . . you are a lot of things, but you are not a traitor," Azula said.

Then she added slyly, "are you?"

I was not going to listen to her twisted words. "Release him immediately!" I shouted to the Dai Li. But of course they did not pay attention to me.

"It's not too late for you, Zuko," Azula pressed on. "You can still redeem yourself."

"The kind of redemption she offers is not for you," Uncle cried out.

"Why don't you let him decide, Uncle? I need you, Zuko, but the only way we win is together. At the end of this day you will have your honor back. You will have Father's love. You will have *everything* you want."

"Zuko, I'm begging you," Uncle said. "Look into your heart and see what it is that you truly want."

"You are free to choose," Azula said. Then she and the Dai Li left.

She is right. I am free to choose. And Uncle is right too. I must look into my heart and find what it is I truly want. That is easy. It's what I've always wanted. I cannot deny my heart, my heritage, and who I truly am.

I raced from the cell out into an open

courtyard, where Azula was battling Katara and the Avatar. They had reached a stale—mate, and then they were each waiting to see who would strike next.

I did. I sent a fire blast that landed right between them. They were all looking at me, wondering what my next move would be. Good. I will show them my choice, the choice I always knew I would make.

I attacked the Avatar with one fire burst after another. I am Prince Zuko of the Fire Nation, and I will fight beside my sister! Working together, we soon had the upper hand. Then a squad of Dai Li agents showed up to help seal our victory. Eventually, one of Azula's blasts injured the Avatar, and he could no longer fight.

We had won! The Fire Nation had tri—umphed!

All of a sudden someone shot a blast of fire in our path. It was Uncle! He was fighting on the side of the Avatar, against us!

"You've got to get out of here," he shouted to Katara. "I'll hold them off as long as I can."

Then he attacked us as Katara escaped

with the Avatar. Once they were gone, he stopped fighting. The Dai Li quickly Earth-bended a rock cage to hold Uncle.

Uncle looked at me without saying a word. Then he looked away. I can tell he's very disappointed in me. But I had to do what I did.

I followed Azula to the Earth King's throne room. It was empty. The Earth King had fled with the Avatar. Now Azula went up to the throne and sat on it, as if it had been hers all along. I stood beside her.

"We've done it, Zuko," she said. "It's taken a hundred years, but the Fire Nation has conquered Ba Sing Se."

I hear what she says, but I can't share her happiness. "I betrayed Uncle," I said, ashamed of what I had done.

"No, he betrayed you," she replied. "When you return home, Father will welcome you as a war hero."

"But I don't have the Avatar. What if Father doesn't restore my honor?"

"He doesn't need to, Zuko. Today you restored your own honor."

Did I? Did I really restore my honor by siding

with my sister and fighting against my uncle? Or did I betray the only man who has always been there for me?

I don't know. I simply don't know. Somehow what I thought was clearly my destiny isn't so clear anymore.